1 3 5 7 9 10 8 6 4 2

Copyright © John Prater 1999

John Prater has asserted his right under the
Copyright, Designs and Patents Act, 1988,
to be identified as the author of this work

First published in the United Kingdom 1999
by The Bodley Head Children's Books
Random House, 20 Vauxhall Bridge Road, London SW1V 2SA

Random House Australia (Pty) Limited
20 Alfred Street, Milsons Point, Sydney
New South Wales 2061, Australia

Random House New Zealand Limited
18 Poland Road, Glenfield
Auckland 10, New Zealand

Random House South Africa (Pty) Limited
Endulini, 5A Jubilee Road,
Parktown 2193, South Africa

Random House UK Limited Reg. No. 954009

A CIP catalogue record for this book
is available from the British Library

ISBN 0 370 32378 5

Printed in Singapore

Number One, Tickle Your Tum

by John Prater

THE BODLEY HEAD
LONDON

Shall we play the

counting game?

Number one

tickle your tum.

Number two

just say 'BOO!'

Number three

touch your knee.

Number four

touch the floor.

Number five

do a dive.

Number six

wiggle your hips.

Number seven

jump to heaven.

Number eight

stand up straight.

Number nine

walk in line.

Number ten

start again.

What a clever

little bear!